PONY GAMES

Rosie Heywood
Designed by Ian McNee

Illustrated by Mikki Rain

Photographs by Kit Houghton

Consultant: Juliet Mander BHSII

Series Editor: Felicity Brooks
Managing Designer: Mary Cartwright
Additional photographs by Bob Langrish
Additional designs by Martin Aggett

Contents

WHAT ARE PONY GAMES?

Pony games, most often called gymkhanas, are riding competitions which involve different races and games. They are often part of larger shows where other events such as jumping take place. The games may look simple, but each one is designed to test you and your pony's skill and training. Taking part is a lot of fun, and a good way to improve your riding skills.

GYMKHANA COMPETITIONS

Why enter gymkhanas?

- Taking part in gymkhanas is a good introduction to competitive riding.
- You will have the motivation to train and practice regularly.
- You will have clear goals to work toward.
- Your riding skills will improve.
- You and your pony will get in better shape.
- You may meet new friends who have the same interests as you.

There are many different types of gymkhnanas. Originally they were held in farmers' fields, for people of all ages. As other more specialized events developed, such as dressage and three-day eventing, gymkhanas became popular with younger riders on ordinary ponies. Local gymkhanas still exist, but there are also more serious competitions which require excellent riding skills. Some competitions are open to individuals, while others are for teams.

Because there are so many types of gymkhanas, it means that there's something suitable for everyone, regardless of age or experience.

In Great Britain, Pony Club teams compete for the Prince Philip Cup, one of the most highly prized gymkhana trophies.

FINDING OUT MORE ABOUT GYMKHANAS

Your local riding school may run an annual gymkhana which riders can enter on school ponies. Joining your local branch of the Pony Club is also an excellent way to find out about gymkhanas. You can sometimes pick up information about local gymkhanas from feed stores and tack shops.

Gymkhanas are normally divided into classes according to age group. Each class has a number of different games. The gymkhana schedule will tell you if you have to send an entry form to the organizer in advance, or whether you can simply enter on the day.

Young riders can enter the games in a lead rein class.

ENTERING A GYMKHANA

It's a good idea to go to watch a few gymkhanas before you enter one. This will give you the chance to see the kinds of games which are included.

When you've watched a few, try entering one or two games in a small, local event. One of the officials should explain the rules before each game begins, but if you are unsure about anything, don't be afraid to ask questions.

In speed games you have to ride as fast as you can, often tackling obstacles on the way.

Precision games involve an element of skill, such as picking up and balancing objects.

GAMES PONIES

Games ponies come in all shapes and sizes. There is no particular breed which does better than others, and a good temperament is more important than the way a pony looks. Experienced games ponies that have won a lot of competitions are very expensive, but every pony has the potential to do well at gymkhnana games.

YOUR PONY'S TEMPERAMENT

If a pony is going to be successful, he must have a good temperament. This means that he behaves well, and has a good attitude toward other ponies and riders.

Calmness

Your pony should be able to stay calm, even when equipment is being waved close to his head. Timid, nervous ponies won't cope with these conditions.

Willingness

He should enjoy competing as much as you do, and be willing to learn. Lazy ponies don't enjoy gymkhanas and they don't usually win many ribbons.

Good behavior

It's important that he's well behaved around other ponies and enjoys their company. He should also be easy to handle, load, shoe and catch.

Intelligence

As you become more experienced, it's important that your pony is intelligent. An intelligent pony will enjoy the different games and will watch the starter's flag as eagerly as you do.

Tolerance

He should be able to put up with you moving around in the saddle as you reach out for pieces of gymkhana equipment. He shouldn't mind if, in the excitement of the gymkhana, your riding is less than perfect.

HOW OLD IS YOUR PONY?

You can tell a pony's age by looking carefully at its teeth. A young pony will have small, white, straight teeth, while an old pony's teeth will be long, discolored and sloping.

An ideal first games pony can be any age from eight to eighteen. Some ponies even continue to compete when they are well into their twenties or beyond. The only hard and fast rule is that ponies under five years old cannot be entered. This is because competing would be too stressful for them, and could strain their developing muscles and bones.

 5 year old

 7 year old
Hook appears.

 10 year old
Hook goes and groove starts.

20 year old
Groove lengthens.

YOUR PONY'S SIZE

You will have chosen your pony so that he's big enough to last you for a few years, but not so big that he's too strong for you.

It's worth bearing in mind the size of your pony when you choose which games to enter. A larger pony will tend to be faster, while a smaller pony will

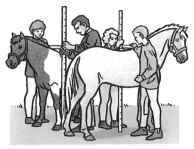

The withers are the highest part of a pony's back.

be more agile and easier to mount and dismount. Ponies are measured in hands and inches from the ground to the withers. A hand is 4in (10cm).

In Pony Club mounted game competitions, there are three divisions of pony size and corresponding rider weight.

YOUR PONY'S CONFORMATION

Your pony's conformation is his shape and the way he is made. A games pony doesn't need to have the kind of conformation which would win him first prize in a showing class, but there are a few important points to look out for.

A good games pony will look athletic, supple and alert.

He should have muscular hindquarters as this is where his speed mainly comes from.

He should have strong legs and healthy feet to take the impact of his movement.

He needs a broad chest and deep girth to allow plenty of room for his heart and lungs.

TRAINING YOUR PONY

Good games ponies can stop and start easily, stay completely still on command and turn tight corners quickly. Normal schooling won't develop these skills, so ask your instructor to help you, and do plenty of practice. The amount of training and practice you'll need depends on you and your pony's experience, and levels of fitness.

BUILDING UP FITNESS

Before you start training your pony, you must make sure he is fit. Sudden stops, starts and sharp turns put strain on his legs, so it's important they are strong. Cantering makes his heart and lungs work hard, so, just like a human athlete, he needs exercises that will build up his fitness gradually.

When your pony is in good shape he will be able to compete in gymkhanas without getting too hot or puffed out.

Gymkhana games test your pony's physical fitness and training.

Fitness program

If your pony has not been working, it will take at least 8 weeks to get him fit.

Spend weeks 1 to 3 just walking. Build up the distance until you can ride him for two hours.

In week 3 start trotting work. Gradually increase the distance.

In week 5 introduce short canters and begin schooling work (see below and right).

In weeks 6 to 8 increase the speed and distance of canters, and schooling.

EXERCISES FOR SUPPLENESS

When your pony is reasonably fit, circling exercises will improve his suppleness and help him to turn quickly. Start with large 20m (66ft) circles. Gradually decrease the size of the circles to 10m (33ft). Start with the slower paces and keep your aids light but clear. Circle in both directions, so your pony doesn't become stiff on one side.

Work on controlling your pony's hindquarters as he turns, so that he doesn't knock equipment with his hind legs.

Put your inside leg on the girth to encourage your pony to bend.

Put your outside leg behind the girth to control his hindquarters.

TRANSITION EXERCISES

A games pony has to stand still at the start of a race, or a false start may be given. He should then move forward at a canter, and be able to stop when you ask him. These changes of pace are called transitions. You need to practice them until your pony responds to the slightest aid. Start with easier transitions such as halt to walk. Try practicing while you're out riding as well as in the school.

For a halt to canter transition, lean forward to prepare for the burst of speed. Use your inside leg on the girth and your outside leg just behind it. Keep the contact on your pony's mouth very light.

For a canter to halt transition, sit taller and deeper in the saddle. Keep your heels down and use your seat to slow your pony down. Close your fingers on the reins and squeeze on his mouth.

VOICE AIDS

Don't forget to talk to your pony. Most gymkhanas allow you to use your voice, so reinforce your leg and hand aids with simple commands such as "Whoa" and "Stand". A clever pony will soon learn to listen. Always talk to him quietly. If you shout he may become alarmed.

IMPROVING BALANCE

A games pony needs good balance to perform well. The circling and transition exercises described above will help to improve your pony's balance. While you do them, encourage him to work actively and not "slop along". By keeping your legs closed gently on his sides and a light contact on his mouth, your pony should engage his hocks. This means he will push himself along with his back legs. Keep as still as you can on his back while you are practicing. Any unnecessary movements may confuse him because he'll have to try to balance you as well.

This pony has his hocks well engaged. As a result, he is pushing himself forward with plenty of energy.

TRAINING WITH EQUIPMENT

Games equipment may be scary for your pony at first, but you can show him there's nothing to worry about. Set out equipment such as barrels, sacks and flags in your schooling area and work around them. Keep both hands on the reins and be ready in case he shies away. Get a helper to show your pony the equipment while you are riding him and talk to him in a reassuring voice. If he seems unworried, ask your helper to pass the equipment to you. Your helper should be ready to hold his head if necessary. If he remains calm, then ride at a walk while holding the equipment. He's most likely to "spook" when you're leaning over to pick equipment up, so practice this movement. Be patient and never rush him.

Equipment tips

Start in an enclosed area with an experienced helper in case things go wrong.

As you ride, keep the equipment still and low at first. He may panic if he sees it above his head.

Try to keep his training as varied as possible.

Some ponies are less confident in strange surroundings, so practice away from home too.

Make sure your pony is familiar with all the equipment and situations he's likely to encounter.

NECK REINING

Neck reining is a way of controlling your pony with one hand. It's a useful technique to learn because it leaves your other hand free to hold equipment.

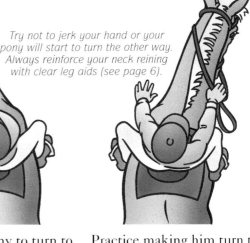

Try not to jerk your hand or your pony will start to turn the other way. Always reinforce your neck reining with clear leg aids (see page 6).

To neck rein, tie a knot in your reins above your pony's withers. Hold the reins with one hand over the knot and your palm down. Hold your hand higher than usual.

To ask your pony to turn to the left, move your hand smoothly over to the left, until he can feel the pressure of the right rein on his neck.

Practice making him turn to the right by moving your hand smoothly over to the right, until he can feel the pressure of the left rein on his neck.

LEADING

You'll have to lead your pony in some races. Once he's leading well at a walk, try leading at different paces. Make sure he doesn't overtake you, as he'll become hard to steer. Teach him to stop when you say "Whoa". With practice, he'll naturally match his pace to yours.

Tips for leading

Stay by his shoulder to encourage him to keep up.

Try not to let him follow behind you as he may run into you.

Use your voice to urge him to "Trot".

Try not to pull him, or turn to look at him.

If your pony is lazy, tap him behind his girth to make him trot.

RIDING SKILLS

Mounted games are fun, but hard work. You'll need to dismount and mount while your pony is moving, reach for equipment and run fast. In order to win, you should be as well trained and fit as your pony. Your first goal should be to improve your fitness with the exercises below, then practice riding skills, such as vaulting, which will speed up your performance.

STRETCHING EXERCISES

Stretch your arms up, then bend to touch your right foot with your right hand. Stretch up again, then touch the other foot. Repeat with your left hand.

Stand up in the stirrups. Put one hand on the pommel to steady yourself and stretch up as far as you can with your other hand. Repeat with the other arm.

Bend slowly back until you are lying on your pony's hindquarters. Try not to let your legs slip forward, though. Return slowly to a sitting position.

With your arms stretched out, swing around to face one side, then the other. Try to do this with a smooth rhythm, keeping your legs as still as you can.

IMPROVING YOUR BALANCE

Improving your balance will help you to keep the correct position in the saddle while you ride at a high speed. You can work on your balance by riding without stirrups or without reins. When you ride without stirrups, cross them over the front of the saddle, so they don't bump against your pony's sides. When you ride without reins, an instructor will need to control your pony using a longe line.

Ask your instructor for a longe lesson. It will help you to improve your balance.

Sit deep in the saddle and relax into your pony's movement. Concentrate on your riding position.

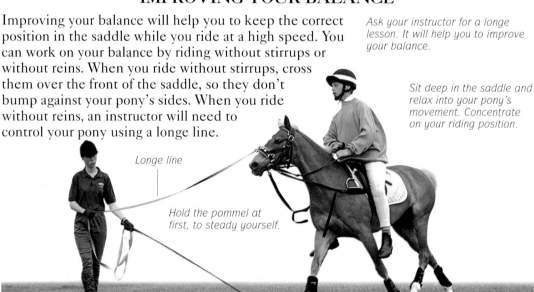

Longe line

Hold the pommel at first, to steady yourself.

FLYING DISMOUNTS

As you approach a task or obstacle, you can save time by dismounting from your pony before he slows down. This is called a flying dismount. It's more usual to dismount on the nearside, but try practicing your flying dismount on the offside too.

Dismount normally, but push out strongly, so you land away from your pony.

As soon as your feet touch the ground, face forward and start running.

Keep your right hand on your pony's neck to steady yourself if you need to.

LEARNING HOW TO VAULT

Vaulting is a way of mounting your pony while he is moving. Learning how to vault takes a little practice, but it's worth the effort because it's much quicker than mounting in the usual way. Make sure your pony is trotting or cantering before you vault, as it is this forward movement that will carry you into the saddle.

This experienced rider is practicing her vault on the offside at a canter.

Urge your pony into a trot or canter and run beside him. Hold the reins in the hand nearest his head. Rest this hand against his neck.

With the other hand, grip the far saddle flap. Watch your pony's stride. As his near front foot hits the ground, jump up.

As you jump, put your weight on the arm holding the saddle and swing your inside leg over the back of the saddle.

TEAM TRAINING

If you've taken part in a few gymkhanas and enjoyed them, the next step may be to join a mounted games team. Most Pony Club branches and some riding schools have a team squad. The squad consists of a number of riders and ponies from which the team is selected.

BEING IN A TEAM SQUAD

Being a member of a team squad is one of the best ways to improve your mounted games skills. You and your pony will become fit and well trained through attending regular practices, and you will learn useful tips from more experienced members. You will also get the chance to enter plenty of competitions, many of them on a more serious level than local gymkhanas.

Training is often more fun when there are other people to keep you company and spur you on.

TEAM PONIES

If your pony enjoys being with other ponies, and doesn't kick or bite, then he'll probably work well in a team. It's also an advantage if he can wait patiently behind the starting line while other ponies are racing, and is willing to lead other ponies and be led. If your pony doesn't have all these qualities, don't worry. As long as he's good-natured, he will gain them with experience.

Each team has five riders who are picked from the squad. The rider who races last wears a white hat band.

CHANGEOVERS

Many team games involve a changeover where equipment is handed from one team member to the next who then continues the race. It's worth practicing changeovers with your teammates until you can do them quickly and accurately. If you're fumbling with equipment, or trying to keep your pony under control, you may lose valuable time.

Watch each other carefully. The incoming pony must have all four feet across the line before the changeover takes place.

Hold the equipment upright by one end so your teammate can take it easily.

Practice both receiving equipment and passing it on.

COMMON PROBLEMS WITH TEAMWORK

Backing off

Backing off can be a problem at changeovers.

If your pony backs off when another pony approaches at high speed, keep him behind the starting line and walk him forward for the changeover. He won't be able to step back.

Shying

Ponies often shy because they lack confidence.

If your pony shies at the changeover, stand a steady pony alongside him. You won't be able to do this in competitions though. Ask the incoming rider to walk toward you at first.

Leading

If your pony dislikes being led by another rider, ask a friend to lead him on a lead rope while you stay in the saddle. Push him on firmly with your legs. Urge him into trot and then a canter.

EQUIPMENT

It's a good idea to build up a collection of gymkhana equipment, so you can practice whenever you want to. Many games use household items which are easily available. Other pieces of equipment, such as flags, are easy and cheap to make.

USING BOTTLES

You can make equipment for the bottle race using plastic bottles. Part fill large empty plastic bottles with sand to weigh them down. You could cover the bottles with brightly colored insulating tape to strengthen them.

Wind tape around bottle.

Sand

In the bottle race you have to pick up plastic bottles from the top of an upturned bin.

Picking up litter

In the litter race you have to pick up pieces of "litter" from the ground without dismounting.

To make the pieces of litter, use large empty plastic bottles, cut off at the "shoulders". To pick the litter up, use a 3ft. wooden dowel.

Hold the dowel about halfway along as it will be easier to control.

Bend as low as you can. Push the end of the dowel into the litter then bring the dowel up carefully so the litter stays on the end.

MAKING YOUR OWN BENDING POLES

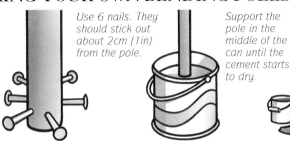

Use 6 nails. They should stick out about 2cm (1in) from the pole.

Support the pole in the middle of the can until the cement starts to dry.

Broom handles or 4ft. 6in. lengths of 1in. PVC pipe make good bending poles. Bamboo canes are not suitable, as they can snap and splinter. Metal posts can injure your pony. You will need five bending poles for a race lane, spaced between 7 and 9m (20-30ft.) apart.

If you use broom handles, ask an adult to help you bang nails into one end of each stick.

Set each pole in a 1 gallon paint can filled with wet cement. Leave until the cement has set.

Paint bright stripes on the poles. You can find out more about bending pole races on page 17.

HOW TO MAKE FLAGS

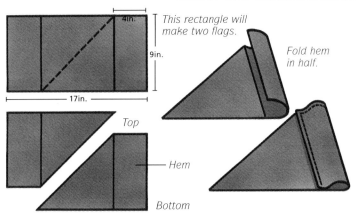

4in.

This rectangle will make two flags.

9in.

Fold hem in half.

17in.

Top

Hem

Bottom

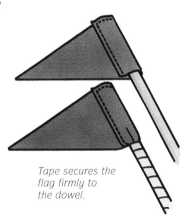

Tape secures the flag firmly to the dowel.

To make triangular flags cut a 9in. by 17in. rectangle of fabric. Draw a straight line 4in. from each short side to make a square. Cut diagonally across the square to make two flags.

Fold each 4in. hem in half, as shown, then sew along the inside edges of the hems and along the tops. Leave the bottoms open so that you have a tube for the wooden dowels to fit into.

Insert a wooden dowel into the tube of each flag. Secure the flags to the dowels with tape. To make rectangular shaped flags attach 6in. by 8in. pieces of cloth to wooden dowels.

A PRACTICE AREA

Set up your practice area in a small field, but not where your pony lives, as it will spoil his grass. Choose a flat, well drained area, as ground that is uneven or wet can be dangerous for your pony. Mark out a race lane 65m (71yds) long. If you're practicing with friends, the distance between lanes should be 7.5m (8yds).

One long pace is about 1m (1yd).

15

SPEED GAMES

When you compete in a speed game, you will have to get from one end of the arena to the other and back again as fast as you can. The speed games described on these pages are traditional favorites, so it's likely that most gymkhanas or mounted games competitions would include at least one of them.

STEPPING STONE DASH

This game involves riding to the end of the arena then back to a row of "stepping stones". You have to dismount, run along the stones then vault back onto your pony and ride to the finish. Dismount well before the stepping stones, so your pony is into a good trotting rhythm and you can quickly vault back onto him when you've run along the stones.

SACK RACE

In the sack race, you have to ride as fast as you can to a marker at the end of the arena, then back to the center line where you dismount and get into a sack. You then have to run or jump to the finish, while leading your pony. It's worth practicing racing in a sack at home. Try jumping along, or sticking your toes in the corners of the sack and shuffling along.

Try not to lean against your pony for support or you may be disqualified.

Keep the sack over your knees.

CANTER, TROT AND WALK

In this game, you and your pony have to race up and down the arena, changing down through the paces when you reach colored markers. If you break the correct pace, you must circle on the spot before continuing. You will need good riding skills to make your pony stay at the correct pace in all the excitement of the race.

ROPE RACE

The rope race is played in teams. You and a partner bend in and out a line of poles, each holding the end of a piece of rope. You should both be able to neck rein (see page 9) so that you can bend through the poles one handed. If you drop the rope, or miss a pole, you must return to the point where you made the mistake. When you reach the finish, one of you picks up another teammate and starts again.

Lean into the poles and use your body weight to guide your pony around each one.

BENDING RACE

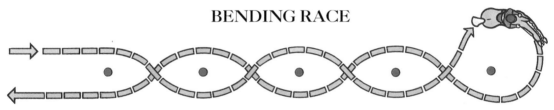

Go wide around the last pole, so that you can ride close to the first post on the return journey.

In the bending race, you have to weave through five upright poles as quickly as you can. If you miss a pole, you must go back and correct your mistake, and if you knock a pole over, you must dismount and put it back up. The bending race forms the basis for several other games including postman's chase and the rope race.

POSTMAN'S CHASE

Postman's chase is always played as a team game. The fifth member of your team stands at the far end of the arena, holding four cardboard "letters". You have to bend through the poles holding a sack, collect one of the letters and put it in the sack, then race back through the bending poles. You must then hand the sack to the next rider who races off to collect another letter.

Go around the back of your teammate after you've collected the letter.

PRECISION GAMES

Precision games involve more than just speed. You
will also have to perform a skill, such as balancing a mug
on top of a pole, or putting a ball in a bucket. Remember
that if you make a mistake, you'll have to go back and
correct it, so it's worth taking a little extra time to carry
out the skill correctly the first time.

THE FLAG RACE

This is one of the most
popular gymkhana games,
with several different
versions. You will have to
take a flag from one
container and put it into
another at high speed,
without dismounting.

*When you collect the flag from the
first container, change your grip so
you're holding it like a sword. This
will give you more control when
you put it into the next container.*

BALL AND CONE RACE

In this game you have to place a tennis
ball on top of a plastic cone, or transfer it
from one cone to another. You won't be
able to balance the ball on the cone while
your pony is cantering, so sit
taller and deeper
in the saddle
and use your
aids to slow
him down.

*Pick the ball up
with your palm
facing backward,
so that if you
fumble, the ball
will fall back into
your hand.*

BALL AND BUCKET RACE

In the ball and bucket race, you have to
ride to the far end of the arena, dismount,
pick up one of four tennis balls, then
remount and ride to the center line to drop
the ball into a bucket. You
must then go get another
ball. When all the
balls are in the
bucket you
can ride to
the finish.

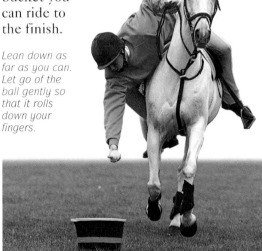

*Lean down as
far as you can.
Let go of the
ball gently so
that it rolls
down your
fingers.*

BALLOON RACE

In this game, there is a board on the center line to which several balloons are attached. At the far end of the arena there is a bin containing a wooden pole with a pin attached to one end. You have to ride to the bin, get the pole, then ride back and burst all the balloons before you cross the finish line. You must remain mounted at all times. This game is often played in teams, with each rider bursting one balloon before passing the pole to the next team member.

Make sure your pony is used to the sight and sound of bursting balloons before you enter the balloon race, otherwise he may become frightened.

MUG RACE

There are several versions of the mug race, one of which involves picking up mugs, one at a time, from an upturned can at the end of the arena, then placing them on top of a row of bending poles. Place each mug gently on the pole. If you slam them down too hard, they may bounce off when you let go.

The mug race involves a lot of changes in speed. When you've collected a mug, canter as fast as you can to the poles, then slow down while you place the mug.

PYRAMID RACE

In this game you have to pick up sand-filled plastic boxes from one table and pile them on top of each other on another table. You don't have to dismount or vault back onto your pony in this race, unless you drop a box and have to pick it up.

Use clear legs aids to keep your pony close to the table.

TACK AND TURNOUT

The Pony Club has firm rules about what you and your pony should wear for competitions. Local gymkhanas are unlikely to be so strict, but check the rules in the schedule. Pony Club games start with a tack (also called saddlery) and turnout inspection. Ribbons are awarded for the neatness and condition of pony, rider and tack.

DRESS AND TACK FOR PONY CLUB COMPETITIONS

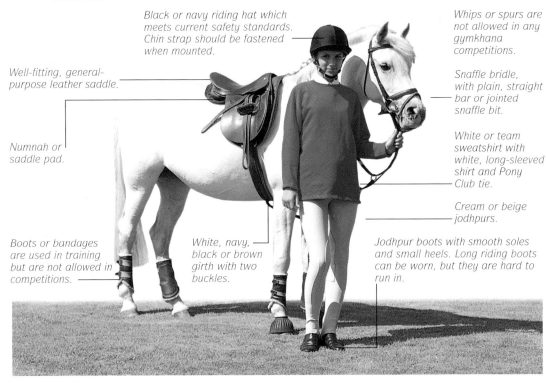

Black or navy riding hat which meets current safety standards. Chin strap should be fastened when mounted.

Whips or spurs are not allowed in any gymkhana competitions.

Well-fitting, general-purpose leather saddle.

Snaffle bridle, with plain, straight bar or jointed snaffle bit.

Numnah or saddle pad.

White or team sweatshirt with white, long-sleeved shirt and Pony Club tie.

Cream or beige jodhpurs.

Boots or bandages are used in training but are not allowed in competitions.

White, navy, black or brown girth with two buckles.

Jodhpur boots with smooth soles and small heels. Long riding boots can be worn, but they are hard to run in.

CHECKING THE SADDLE

Check the fit of your pony's saddle regularly, as this is one of the things that tack inspection judges look for. A badly fitting saddle could also harm your pony. Make sure the saddle lies flat on his back with the weight evenly distributed.

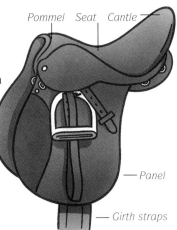

Pommel Seat Cantle

Panel

Girth straps

Gap

You should be able to see a clear gap between your pony's spine and the saddle.

Pommel

You should be able to fit four fingers between the pommel of the saddle and your pony's withers.

NOSEBANDS

There are several different types of nosebands. Apart from the cavesson (see below), most nosebands are pieces of corrective tack. They are designed to make a strong pony easier to control by preventing him from opening his mouth.

Always ask an experienced person for advice if you think your pony needs any kind of corrective tack, including nosebands. Cavesson, flash, drop or grakle nosebands are all allowed in gymkhana and mounted games competitions.

Cavesson

Cavesson nosebands improve the look of a pony's head. They are available in different widths, to suit different breeds of ponies.

Drop

If you use a drop noseband, make sure it is fitted correctly. If it is too low, it could restrict your pony's breathing.

Flash

Make sure the top strap of a flash noseband is tight enough not to slip down and interfere with your pony's breathing.

Grakle

Cheek-bone

A grakle noseband stops the pony from crossing his lower jaw. Make sure it does not fit too high or it may rub the pony's cheekbones.

CHECKING THE FIT OF THE BRIDLE

The bit should stick out of your pony's mouth about ½cm (¼in) on each side. Make sure you can fit your forefingers between the ends of the bit and the sides of his mouth.

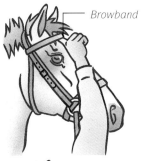

Browband

The browband should sit just below your pony's ears, but not touching them. It must fit closely, but make sure it is not so tight that it pulls the bridle forward.

Throat latch

When the throat latch is fastened, it should be loose enough to allow your pony to breathe easily. You should be able to fit your fist inside it.

You should be able to get two fingers between a cavesson noseband and your pony's face. The noseband should sit four fingers below his cheekbones.

USING MARTINGALES

Running and standing martingales are pieces of corrective tack which prevent ponies from throwing their heads up and becoming out of control. You are allowed to use a standing martingale in gymkhanas and mounted games, but it will need to be fitted carefully, so ask an experienced person to help you at first. Remember that adding a martingale is not the cure for a problem and that good schooling with a qualified instructor is far better than corrective tack.

Standing martingale

The standing martingale strap should be loose enough to reach up to the throat.

Running martingale

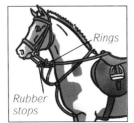

Rings

Rubber stops

Stops on a running martingale prevent the rings slipping toward the bit.

The rings should be one hand's length from the withers when you pull them back.

BOOTS AND BANDAGES

Boots and bandages protect your pony's lower legs from injuries and give them support. They can be worn when training but are not allowed in competitions. Boots should be fastened securely so that they do not come loose. Boot buckles fasten on the outside of your pony's legs, pointing backward. Bandages should be tight enough not to slip, but if they are too tight, they will be uncomfortable for him.

Types of boots

Over-reach boots protect your pony's front heels from being stepped on by his hind feet.

Brushing boots prevent your pony knocking his opposite legs together. They also give general protection against bumps.

Tendon boots can be covered or open-fronted. They protect the pony's tendons at the back of his lower legs.

Putting on exercise bandages

Wrap gauze padding around the lower leg. Start bandaging just below the knee (or hock). Fold the free end down and bandage over it.

Continue to wind the bandage evenly down to the fetlock. Work back up to the top, until you reach the tapes at the end of the bandage.

Tie the end tapes around the leg and tuck them under a fold. Sew over the fold or wrap plastic insulating tape around it, so the bandage can't come undone.

STUDS

Studs fit into special holes in your pony's shoes and stop him from slipping on very hard or wet ground. You will need to ask the farrier to include the holes in your pony's shoes. Take the studs out after competing and fill the holes with keepers or cotton covered with vaseline to stop small stones from blocking them.

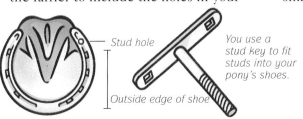

Stud hole

Outside edge of shoe

You use a stud key to fit studs into your pony's shoes.

Pointed studs are used for hard ground.

Square studs are only used when the ground is very wet.

TAKING CARE OF TACK

It's important to clean your tack regularly, ideally after every ride. Wash, dry and rub the leather parts of the saddle and bridle with saddle soap to keep the leather soft and supple. Ordinary soap would make it hard and dry. Scrub fabric girths and halters with soap and water. Avoid detergents as they may irritate your pony's skin. Make sure your pony's saddle pad or numnah is clean too. Remove the bit from the bridle and clean it thoroughly in very hot water after every ride. Do not use soap, as your pony may react badly to a soapy taste in his mouth.

Tack checklist

- Always keep your tack clean and in good repair.
- Check that the stitching on the girth, stirrup leathers, reins and bridle is not broken or frayed.
- Check all the leather for cracks and signs of wear.
- Check the bit carefully for any signs of roughness.
- Check that the saddle and bridle fit your pony correctly (see pages 20 & 21).
- Make sure any boots or bandages fit your pony correctly and are firmly fastened.

If you look after your tack carefully, it should last for many years.

GETTING READY

As the day of the gymkhana approaches, you will need to decide how to get to the showground. If the show is nearby, it may be best to ride there, but if it is far away you will need a horse van or trailer. Before you set off, prepare your pony and check that you have everything you'll need.

PREPARING YOUR PONY

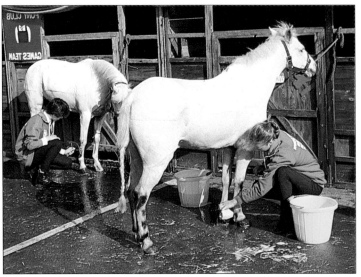

Wash muddy legs with warm water then dry them thoroughly.

Groom your pony thoroughly before the gymkhana, so that he looks his best.

Pick out his feet and use a dandy brush to remove mud and loose hair from his coat. Body brush him all over to remove grease and dirt, then sponge his eyes, nose and bottom with separate sponges. Brush his mane and tail in small sections to remove tangles. Finally, polish his coat with a stable cloth to make it shine and paint his hooves with plenty of hoof oil.

RIDING TO THE SHOW

If you are riding to the gymkhana, plan your route well in advance. There are very few bridle trails in the country, so you will probably have to ride on the road for most if not all of your journey.

If possible, ask someone with a car to meet you at the show and bring the things you will need, such as your grooming kit. Allow plenty of time for your journey. If the showground takes more than half an hour to get to at a walk and steady trot, you should arrange to go by horse van or trailer.

If you are not being met at the show, pack a small backpack with a halter, a lead rope, a blanket, a hoof pick, a body brush, a first aid kit and some money.

Road Safety tips

• Make sure your pony is used to vehicles before you take him on the road.
• Always keep to the right.
• Wear a reflective bib so you can be seen easily.
• Raise your hand, or nod and smile, to thank motorists who slow down.
• Wait for a clear road before passing any scary objects.
• Ride with an adult or experienced friend.
• Learn your Highway Code.
• Take your Pony Club riding and road safety examination.

PROTECTIVE CLOTHING

When your pony travels in a horse van or trailer, he needs special clothing to keep him warm and to protect him against accidental knocks.

Stable wraps should cover the fetlocks. You can also use shipping boots, which are padded wraps with velcro straps.

A tail guard, with a tail bandage underneath, protects the tail.

Thick leather hock boots protect the hocks from bumps.

Blankets keep the pony warm. Use a sweat sheet under a summer sheet if it's warm, or a wool day blanket if it's cold.

Knee boots protect the knees from knocks.

TRAILERS AND HORSE VANS

If your pony is traveling to the gymkhana in a trailer or horse van, practice loading and unloading him a few days before the journey. An experienced person will need to show you what to do and help you on the day. Make sure the floor is covered with bedding or rubber matting to prevent your pony from slipping. Hang up a haynet for him to nibble on the way and take a container full of water so you can give him drinks. Your pony needs lots of fresh air, so open the vents of the horse van or trailer.

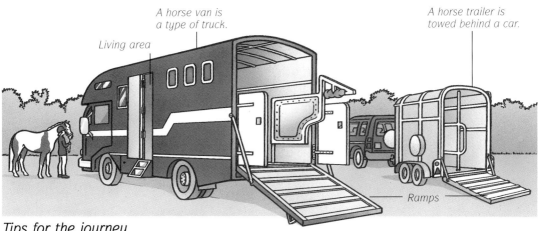

A horse van is a type of truck.

Living area

A horse trailer is towed behind a car.

Ramps

Tips for the journey
- Plan a long journey so the only breaks you need are to check on your pony.
- Stop in a safe place such as a service area.

- It is dangerous and illegal to be with the pony when the horse van is moving, so always stop the vehicle to check on your pony.

- Keep stops as short as possible and try not to unsettle your pony.
- On a long journey, offer your pony small drinks.

AT THE GYMKHANA

Many gymkhanas are part of larger shows, where different events happen throughout the day. There is a lot to do when you arrive, so try to reach the showground in good time. Then you don't have to rush your preparations.

LOOKING AFTER YOUR PONY

If you have ridden to the gymkhana, unsaddle your pony and settle him in the shade, out of the wind. If you have arrived by horse van or trailer, unload him as soon as you arrive. He may be a bit stiff, so lead him around to loosen him up and give him a chance to familiarize himself with his surroundings. Tie him to a piece of string attached to a ring on the trailer. If for any reason he panics and pulls back, the string will break and he won't injure himself. Bring your own water and containers to avoid the risk of infection from troughs at the showground.

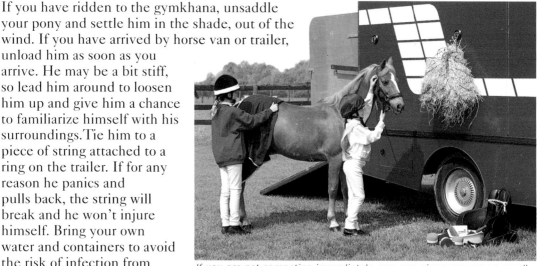

If you are not competing immediately, you can give your pony a small haynet once he's settled.

FINDING YOUR WAY AROUND

When your pony is settled and happy, leave an experienced friend in charge, while you go to find the secretaries' tent. Fill in an entry form if you have not already done so, and check in. Make sure you know what time the first race in your age-class starts. Walk around the showground and find the gymkhana arena, practice ring and warm-up area. You should be aware of the ground conditions when you compete, as very short grass and wet grass can be slippery.

WARMING UP EXERCISES

It's important to warm up before you compete, so that you and your pony are ready for racing. Warming up helps to prevent injuries, as warm muscles are less likely to strain than cold ones. Try the stretching exercises shown for ten minutes, then spend about twenty minutes warming up your pony.

If you rode to the gymkhana, your pony will only need about a ten minute warm-up. Don't work him too hard. You are trying to loosen his muscles, not wear him out.

Stand up straight, then bend down to touch your toes. Straighten up slowly without bending your legs. Repeat five times.

Rotate each arm in forward circles, then backward circles ten times. Finally, jog on the spot for a few minutes.

Stand with your feet apart. Raise your left arm. Bend to the right and straighten up. Raise your right arm and bend to the left.

Warm up your pony with some transitions to put him through his paces. Then try a few stops and starts and do a couple of vaults and flying dismounts.

THE PRACTICE RING

Announcements will probably be made over a loudspeaker. Listen to them carefully, as you will be called to the practice ring before each of your races. Once you are in the ring, pay attention to the steward. He or she may call out people's names before each race to make sure all the contestants are there.

The practice ring can get very crowded and hectic. Try to stay calm.

Tips before you start

• Try not to rush, as this puts you and your pony under stress.
• Relax. If you are nervous your body will be tense and you won't ride at your best.
• Be positive. Negative thinking isn't good for your confidence.
• Keep calm and don't panic, or your pony may become over-excited.
• Just before you go into the arena, close your eyes for a few moments and breathe calmly and deeply.
• Don't forget you're there to enjoy yourself!

COMPETING

When you enter the arena to compete, all your skills and training are tested in just a few intense moments. During the games, concentrate hard on what you are doing and try not to get distracted by the other competitors. Most importantly of all, remember that you've entered the gymknana to have fun and enjoy yourself.

HOW THE ARENA IS SET OUT

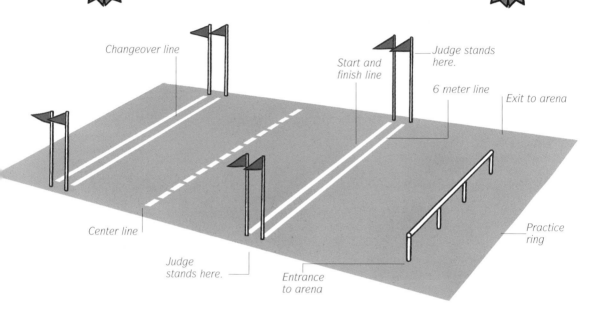

Changeover line

Start and finish line

Judge stands here.

6 meter line

Exit to arena

Center line

Judge stands here.

Entrance to arena

Practice ring

HEATS

If there are a lot of entrants, games are run in heats. The winner of each heat goes through to the final. Watch the other heats in your game, as you may pick up some useful tips. When everyone is ready on the start line, the starting official will lower a white flag to signal the start of the heat.

If one of the riders moves off before the flag is lowered, the starting official will blow a whistle to signal a false start.

Tips for competing

- Remember that accuracy is more important than speed.
- Don't get distracted by other competitors. Concentrate on what you are doing.
- Always correct mistakes, no matter how long it takes.
- Always finish the game, even if you seem to be last. Another rider may be disqualified.
- Don't argue with the judge. His or her decision is final.
- Whether you win or lose, always remember to congratulate your pony.

LINE STEWARDS

In Pony Club mounted games, each race lane has two line stewards, one at each end. At the end of the game, the line stewards tell the judge if an error has been made and not corrected and what that error was. The team is not informed, as this would be unauthorized assistance. Team members are responsible for telling each other if they have spotted an error.

In the U.K., line stewards will notify the team if an error has been made, but this is not allowed in the U.S.

Between games

- Between the games, try to conserve your pony's energy.
- Dismount, and keep him in the shade if it's hot.
- If it's cold, put a blanket over him.
- If there is a long gap between the games you have entered, take him back to the trailer or horse van for a rest.

AT THE END OF THE DAY

Hopefully you will win some ribbons. If you don't, try not to be downhearted. Think about the events you did do well at. Also think about how your general riding skills have improved as a result of your gymkhana training. Pinpoint the weaknesses that let you down, so you can work to improve them before the next time. When you get home, check your pony's legs for any hot patches or bumps. Make sure that he has settled in well after the journey and that he eats a good dinner.

POLO AND OTHER SPORTS

Gymkhana games are an excellent introduction to other competitive mounted sports such as polo and horseball. The skills you learn as part of a mounted games team are very similar to those used in these action-packed sports. Even if you don't get the chance to take part, mounted sports are exciting to watch.

POLO

Polo was first played over three thousand years ago by the tribespeople of Persia and China. In more recent times, polo has become popular in Europe and the Americas.

The object of the game is to score goals by hitting a ball through the goalposts using a long polo stick. Polo is played in seven and a half minute periods called chukkas. The number of chukkas in a match can be between four and eight and is decided beforehand. Because polo is played almost entirely at the gallop, the players change their ponies after every chukka and no pony can play more than two chukkas in a match.

The four team members are given numbers called handicaps. High numbers are given to good players. The handicaps are added up to give the team handicap. This decides which tournaments the team can enter.

Riding off
A polo player will often try to "ride off" an opponent. This means by neck-reining and using firm leg aids, the player pushes his or her pony toward the opponent, forcing him or her to move away from the ball.

Above: Although riding off involves physical contact, penalties are given to players who ride dangerously.

Left: Polo players wear helmets and thick leather knee pads and boots.

HORSEBALL

Horseball is a mixture of rugby and basketball played on horseback. Two teams of six riders play against each other. Only four players from each team are allowed on the pitch at the same time, but substitutions can be made at any point. The game is played in two halves of ten minutes using a ball enclosed in a harness with six leather handles. Players use their hands to catch and pass the ball. Team members have to gain possession of the ball, then pass it at least three times within their team, before attempting to score by shooting the ball through a hoop.

Horseball players learn how to lean out of the saddle in order to pick the ball up from the ground.

The fast pace of the game and the impressive shooting and passing skills of the players make horseball an exciting sport to watch.

POLOCROSSE

Many Pony Club members go on to play polocrosse when they become too old to take part in mounted games. Players throw and catch a soft foam rubber ball, using a long stick that has a net attached to its oval head. The Pony Club plays three divisions of games, divided by age group. The number of team members varies from 2 to 6 depending on the division. A goal is scored when an attacking player uses his or her stick to throw the ball into the goal.

Polocrosse players use their sticks to catch the ball, or pick it up from the ground. They cannot use their hands.

INDEX

With thanks to Pat Mendenhall with the American Pony Club for assistance
with the American edition, Clare Davies, Nicola Leese, Robert Leese,
Charlotte O'Neill, Hannah O'Neill, Hannah Paul, Ben, Dorian, Inca, Kes,
Lady, Speedy, and the Horse Unit at Writtle Agricultural College.